Forever & Always

Cristian Carrington

ISBN: 979-8-218-57354-6
Imprint: Independently published

To my dearest wife, you are my rock, my cheerleader, and the best life partner I could ever ask for. You've been with me through every plot twist and cliffhanger, always ready to offer a snack or a reality check—whichever I need more. Your support means the world to me, and I can't thank you enough for being the reason I keep typing away. You're my forever and always.

To Dabber, thank you for being my personal hype person, always talking up my work and wearing your pride in our friendship on your sleeve. This book is a shoutout to you, as a token of my appreciation. May it be a narrative you cherish—and hey, feel free to brag and say you got a mention now.

To my incredible fans, thank you for every bit of enthusiasm and support. A special shoutout to the listeners of "The Talking Hour Podcast" – knowing you're out there listening and engaging means the world to me. Your willingness to follow my creative journey, from the podcast to the pages of this book, is something I'm truly grateful for.

To my family, who have been my first audience and my lifelong supporters, keep your eyes peeled. The next few books might just have a page with a familiar name. It's a small way to say thank you for the roles you've played in this grand adventure.

Contents

CHAPTER ONE

A DANCE TO REMEMBER

In the embrace of the vast sea, a mysterious tropical island and its three smaller siblings held secrets and wonders. Home to two thousand souls and a life-giving spring, one neighboring isle glittered with precious metals, another teemed with untamed cattle, while the third concealed a miraculous healing plant. Amidst this paradise, a young man was about to embark on an adventure that would become the stuff of legends.

With unparalleled skills as a fisherman, he was the subject of many tales. What made his mastery even more astonishing was his youth; to be the best among seasoned fishers in his mid-twenties was a testament to his prodigious talent.

His skin, as deep as a moonless night, harmonized with his short, well-maintained curls that seemed to carry the intoxicating aroma of ripe mangoes.

Every corner of the town buzzed with whispers about him. Women were especially taken, their eyes often trailing him just a moment longer than usual, each gaze filled with silent hopes and unspoken dreams. But amidst the sea of admirers, his heart sailed in a different direction.

Today was the day he had decided to act on his feelings. Carrying a carefully curated basket of gifts filled with an assortment of exotic fruits and a trinket carved with great care from the timber of his own vessel, he ventured to Laka's home. She lived just up the hillside, a few winding roads away from his own abode. She was a recent addition to this part of the city, having relocated from its deeper, bustling heart. It was an area he rarely ventured into, for his life was bound to the sea.

He knocked on the door, and a wave of nervousness washed over him. He cleared his throat, once, then twice, trying to shake off the jitters. Instinctively, he cupped a hand over his mouth, testing his breath. The sweet scent of pineapples reassured him, and he nodded to himself, mustering up the courage for another knock. But just as his hand was about to tap the door again, it swung open to reveal her. Her eyes, always so full of grace, met his with a calm and steady gaze.

"Lono?" she greeted with a hint of curiosity in her voice.

"I... uh, brought you this," he shoved the basket towards her, "I thought you might like it."

She looked at the basket, then back at him, her lips curving into a gentle smile. "Aww, thank you! That's very thoughtful of you. And what's this?" she asked, pointing to the wooden trinket peeking out from the basket.

"That," he said, his voice taking on a hint of pride, "is a turtle. The wood, it's from my ship."

Her laughter, light and melodic, filled the air. "It's lovely. Thank you very much." Her eyes darted inside the house, scanning for a suitable spot to place the thoughtful gift. "Wanna come inside?" she offered.

He shifted slightly, "Actually, I was hoping to take you out maybe. There's a fire at sunset today by the beach."

Her eyes lit up with excitement. "Yeah, I'm down," she said with a radiant smile.

"So, is it a date?" he asked, pulling a playful face.

"It's a date," she agreed, her voice filled with anticipation. Carefully placing the gift on a nearby sofa, she grabbed two ripe mangoes before heading out. The promise of a beautiful evening ahead lingered in the air.

As the sun began its descent, casting the sky in hues of orange and pink, they made their way to the beach. The soft sand crunched beneath their feet, and the distant sound of waves crashing provided a soothing backdrop to their journey.

Upon reaching the shore, they found a weathered log smoothed by time. They sat down on it. The beach was alive with activity. Families, friends, and lovers gathered, their laughter and chatter blending into a harmonious cacophony. Children ran along the shoreline, their silhouettes playing chase with the retreating waves.

The rhythmic pulse of drums resonated deeply, echoing tales of ancient fishermen, legendary voyages, and the timeless dance of nature. The ukuleles, with their gentle strumming, seemed to flirt with the breeze, creating a melody that was both playful and nostalgic.

Every so often, they would exchange words, but mostly, they sat in comfortable silence, absorbing the beauty around them. The world seemed to slow down, and in that moment, all that mattered was the connection they shared and the magic of the evening.

Having savored the sweetness of mangoes and sipped refreshing coconut water, she turned to him with a playful glint in her eyes. "Would you like to dance?" she inquired, her voice carrying a hint of mischief.

He hesitated for a moment, a mix of excitement and nervousness evident in his gaze. While no stranger to the rhythms of the sea, dancing to the beats of the island was a different challenge altogether.

Seeing his hesitation, she extended her hand, her fingers beckoning with a gentle allure. "Come on," she coaxed with a reassuring smile, "Just let the music guide you."

With every beat, she moved with a grace that seemed to defy the very laws of nature. Her feet tapped the earth with strength and purpose, while her arms flowed through the air, as fluid as the streams that meandered through the valleys. The sway of her hips told stories of ancient traditions, and the twirl of her skirt painted whirlwinds of vibrant colors.

From his vantage point, he was utterly captivated. The way she danced left him in awe, and when their eyes locked, he didn't just see her; it was as if he witnessed the entire forest come alive in her gaze. As the music began to fade, a new melody took its place - the hauntingly beautiful songs of whales echoing from the depths of the ocean. Though his feet remained firmly planted in the sand, the earth beneath him seemed to pulse and sway, joining in their dance.

Their souls, no longer tethered to the ground, began to float, first hovering above the bonfire, illuminating their forms in its fiery glow. Then, lifted by the very winds of the island, they soared, overseeing the vast expanse of their tropical home and the deep blue ocean beyond. As they danced in this ethereal realm, their souls intertwined, melting into one another, evoking a sense of comfort and connection that felt as old as the island itself.

They exchanged smiles between them. With a gentle tug, she pulled him closer, their bodies moving in harmony to the rhythm of the ocean. As they swayed, he glanced down at his arm, which seemed to meld seamlessly with hers. The sight was entrancing: swirls of iridescent colors danced and twirled, creating patterns that were both otherworldly and breathtakingly beautiful. He was witnessing the birth of galaxies and the dance of stars. Amidst this cosmic display, a tiny flower began to blossom from his palm.

His gaze wandered from her, drawn to a distant silhouette against the horizon. There, a pale horse stood, its ribs stark against its frail frame, each step a testament to its lingering will. Its eyes, deep and weary, found his, sharing a silent, knowing exchange. But what unsettled him was not the horse's evident suffering, but the subtle upward curve of its lips. It was a smile, but not one of joy or contentment. The sight left him awash with confusion and a lingering sense of unease, even as he tried to pull his thoughts back towards her.

As he attempted to refocus on her, a voice, ethereal and commanding, whispered, "Come." The word resonated in his ears, sending ripples through his consciousness.

Suddenly, he felt an invisible force gripping his ankle, pulling him away from the moment. His eyes widened in confusion and fear. Laka, sensing his distress and mistaking it for shyness, bent slightly, capturing his gaze with a reassuring smile and a gentle wave. But Lono, now terrified, shook his head vigorously, his eyes screaming a silent "NO."

In an instant, the force yanked him downward, so swiftly that one moment he was locked in Laka's gaze, and the next, he was spiraling down a kaleidoscope-type otherworldly tunnel.

The walls twisted and pulsated as if alive, creating a jarring symphony of visual and auditory sensations that left him feeling overwhelmed. He could sense countless predatory eyes upon him, stripping away his sense of innocence. A sudden urge to cover his body, to shield himself from those unseen watchers, washed over him.

He clenched his eyes shut, desperate to escape the unnerving realm he found himself in. When he dared to open them again, he was met with the familiar sight of the beach, feeling the coolness of the sand beneath him. He was lying on the ground with Laka kneeling beside him, her face etched with concern. A small crowd had gathered around, their expressions a mix of curiosity and worry. The shaman, a figure of wisdom and spiritual guidance in their community, made his way through the crowd, asking everyone to give them some space.

Lono's brain was a whirlwind of confusion, struggling to make sense of the abrupt transition from the surreal tunnel back to the tangible world. His senses were in overdrive, trying to ground themselves, to assure him that he was indeed back to safety.

The shaman, now kneeling adjacent to Laka, looked intently at Lono, his eyes searching for signs of distress. "Are you okay, young one? Can you tell me what you saw?" he asked, his voice gentle yet filled with concern.

Lono, still grappling with the remnants of confusion, looked up at the shaman, his eyes wide. "We were flying... then a horse smiled at me?... then there were..." He paused, sitting up as he spoke, his voice trailing off as he realized how bizarre his experience sounded. He finally admitted, his voice barely above a whisper, almost as if he was afraid of being deemed insane. "I saw eyes looking at me..."

The shaman, his expression thoughtful, nodded slowly. "Come to the temple tomorrow," he suggested gently. "We can discuss this with the other shamans, see if they can make sense of your experience."

Lono stood up, still feeling a bit shaky but grateful for the shaman's concern. "I might just do that," he said, managing a small smile. "Thank you for checking on me."

Turning to Laka, he asked, "Do you want to go for a walk?"

She, who had been quietly observing the exchange, nodded. "I'd like that," she said softly.

And so, they walked away from the fire and the crowd, strolling along the shores of the beach.

He asked if she had seen any horses or experienced anything unusual while they were in the spiritual realm.

"Honestly, no," she responded nonchalantly.

"Do you think it's serious?" she inquired.

"Doubt it. But those eyes were definitely concerning," he admitted.

"Really?" she said, stopping in her tracks. "How do you feel now?"

"Better I guess... Actually, I'm sorry. I'll just check in tomorrow. I'm sure it's nothing," he reassured her, trying to play it off.

"You better. You had me worried back there," she giggled.

He smirked back, "Yeah..." They resumed walking. "By the way... Would you be okay going out with me again?" he asked, his voice tinged with slight nervousness.

"Are you kidding? I would love to," she laughed lightly. "I've never bonded with someone like that before..."

"You're right... I've got you hooked, huh?" he teased.

She nudged him with her elbow, causing him to lose his balance slightly, and they both burst into smiles.

"Ready to head home?" she asked.

"Honestly, I'm kind of tired after all that, so yeah," he replied. They began walking towards her place. "So, what's the secret of the greatest fisherman in these parts?" she asked, her curiosity piqued.

"Bait and love," he declared proudly.

"You're joking, right?" she chuckled.

"No, seriously," he laughed. "The other fishermen, they don't respect the waters like I do."

"Hey, if it works, it works, right?" she agreed.

They had reached her house. "Well, Laka, I had a great time. When can we do this again?" he asked, looking into her eyes.

"I don't know..." she hesitated, causing a flicker of confusion in his eyes. He didn't want to pressure her or ruin the moment. "I'm actually free right now, but I remember you mentioned feeling tired..." she teased, a playful glint in her eyes. His face lit up, unable to hide his excitement, as he flashed the biggest grin of the day. "Tired? Me? Nah, that's not my style," he chuckled. "Oh really?" she playfully interrupted. "Yeah, that's just not me," he continued, laughter still in his voice. "Prove it," she challenged, her voice now with a serious and passionate undertone. She opened her door, extending her hand towards him. His demeanor shifted, his tone now matching hers. He accepted her hands as they made their way inside.

Chapter Two

NEW LIFE

Several months had passed since that memorable night on the beach, and the bond between Lono and Laka had only grown stronger. They were inseparable, spending every possible moment together, their lives intertwined in a dance of love and companionship. Some onlookers whispered, speculating that this intense phase would fade, "Give them a year living together, and they'll be sick of each other," some said. But for now, they were lost in their own world.

A year had indeed passed, and the once unbeatable fisherman of the city, Lono, was far from his former glory. His attention was no longer on the waves and the catch of the day; it was solely on Laka. Her job as a nanny also suffered due to their inseparable nature. They tried to blend their worlds; she accompanied him to sea, but it was to no avail. The first trip resulted in a meager catch; the second left her seasick, with him tending to her instead of fishing; and the third was a near-death disaster, with a misplaced spear almost piercing him. It was clear: their professional lives were suffering.

They decided he would cut his hours at sea, and she would stay home, trying to keep herself busy. But even this arrangement couldn't quell their need for each other. Time apart brought headaches, stress, and a myriad of other symptoms. They were addicted to each other's presence, and it was taking a toll.

Two years into their intense relationship, they had to make a significant change. Lono's house was sold, providing them with a comfortable cushion of funds. They relocated into Laka's smaller, yet cozier place, creating a perfect sanctuary for their love. Now, with all the time in the world to spend together, they eagerly awaited the arrival of a new chapter in their lives.

Laka, comfortably seated on the back porch with a serene view of the sea stretching out before her, gently caressed her pregnant belly, lost in thought. Their house, perched upon a hill, offered a tranquil retreat from the world. Lono, having just returned from a grocery run, placed the baskets in the kitchen and began to search for her.

"Baby?" he called out softly, but there was no response. He walked a bit farther, finally spotting her through the back window. A warm smile spread across his face as he admired her, bathed in the soft glow of the rising sun. Her black skin glowed warmly, and her frizzy, puffed curls surrounded her face like a soft halo. "I am so lucky," he thought to himself, his heart swelling with love and gratitude.

He opened the back door and made his way to her, his presence immediately filling the space with warmth. "Hey my love," he greeted, his hand gently resting on her shoulder. "Hi baby," she responded, tilting slightly for a sweet kiss, which he gladly met.

"Where were you, love?" she inquired, her eyes filled with curiosity.

"I went to pick up a few things for our anniversary tomorrow," he replied, his voice brimming with excitement. "I honestly wasn't expecting you to be up this early," he added, his tone soft.

"Aww, that's so sweet. Thank you, love," she expressed, standing up to stretch a little. "So, what are we having to eat? She's starving," she said, placing a hand on her belly and giggling.

"What?!" he said in mock surprise, kneeling down to talk directly to the baby. "You love eating up my food, huh?" he teased, placing his ear against her belly as if waiting for a reply.

"Our food..." Laka corrected him with a playful smirk.

He pulled back, feigning shock. "Hey, that's what she said, not me," Laka quipped, and they both burst into laughter, the sound echoing with love and happiness.

"Okay, okay, I see how it is," he chuckled, taking her hands in his and gently leading her back inside the house. "For today's feast, we'll be having fish fillet, coconut rice, fried plantains, some sea beans, and a side of soup made from the fish head," he announced with pride.

"Oh my goodness... I cannot wait!" she exclaimed, her eyes lighting up with utmost excitement at the mouthwatering menu he had just described.

The tranquil atmosphere was abruptly shattered by the blaring sound of a loud horn, causing her to startle. "What is that for, hun?" she asked, her voice laced with curiosity.

"That's a warning horn..." he replied, his brow furrowing as he tried to recall what it could signify. "Honestly, I've never actually heard it with my own ears before," he continued, his voice trailing off as he processed the situation.

"Whoa, hopefully everything's okay, right?" she asked, concern evident in her tone.

"Yeah, I'm sure it's... maybe," he was cut off by another blast of the horn, now sounding more urgent. "Oh my. How many times are they gonna do that?" she asked, attempting to lighten the mood and ease his growing concern.

However, his expression only grew more serious. "One's for warning, two is for importance, and the last is for emergency..." he explained as he rushed to the front door, peering out to see people either stepping out of their houses or running towards the shore.

"Babe... Is everything okay out there?" she asked, her voice filled with worry.

"Stay inside, love," he urged, gently nudging her back into the house. Just then, the horn sounded for a third time, its tone now ominous.

"I have to go," he said quickly, planting a swift kiss on her lips. As he turned to leave, she grabbed his arm, stopping him in his tracks.

"Please, love..." she pleaded, her eyes beginning to well up with tears.

"I know, love, but this is exactly why I need to run down there. I have to find out what's happening," he said, his voice firm yet gentle. He extended his pinky finger towards her, and after a moment's hesitation, she locked her pinky with his.

"I promise I'll come back if it's anything crazy, okay?" he assured her. She couldn't bring herself to speak, fearing her voice would betray her emotions, so she simply nodded in agreement and gave him another kiss.

With that, Lono, now in full alert mode, ran down towards the shore, his heart racing not just from the exertion, but also from the uncertainty of what could be so important to warrant an emergency classification. He couldn't shake the thought from his mind: the horns had never been sounded three times before. What could possibly be happening?

CHAPTER THREE

THEY CAME BEARING GIFTS

Laka, driven by curiosity and a hint of fear, decided to venture out to the back of the house to catch a glimpse of what was happening at the beach. Her face contorted into a mix of confusion and fear as she laid eyes on the sight before her. She had heard countless stories, tales, and adventures of her people, all concluding that their world was isolated, surrounded by endless seas in every direction. The idea of there being more was unfathomable.

What she saw were three ships, one of which was significantly larger than the others, adorned with a giant horse figurehead at its prow. Each ship dwarfed any structure her community had ever built. "How many people can fit in there?" she wondered aloud, estimating that each ship could easily hold a few hundred people.

Meanwhile, Lono was making his way towards the shore, his pace quickening as the ships came into full view. With each house he passed, he caught glimpses of the vessels, but now they were displayed in all their grandeur. He reached the top of the last hill, and as he looked down, he saw nearly all the males from the island gathered at the shore. Some were engaged in hushed conversations, others brandished weapons, and a few mothers stood by with their children. Beyond them all were the massive ships.

"By the Gods," he whispered to himself, standing there in awe, trying to comprehend the magnitude of what he was witnessing.

"Lono!" a voice called out amidst the commotion, cutting through the air. Lono turned his head, recognizing the voice instantly.

"Bomoh!" Lono called back, making his way through the crowd to reach him.

Bomoh, the shaman who had helped him a couple of years prior, was surrounded by the city's elders and other shamans.

"What's happening?" Lono asked, urgently.

Bomoh gestured for the others to continue towards the beach, then turned to Lono. "We're not sure yet. Is Laka okay?" he asked, concern in his eyes.

"Yeah, she's at home," he replied quickly, his mind racing. "I thought we were alone in this world," he muttered, his voice filled with disbelief.

"We all did. Now, we can only hope their intentions are honest and peaceful," Bomoh said, placing a reassuring hand on Lono's shoulder.

"Yeah, let's hope," Lono responded, though he couldn't shake the feeling of unease. Together, they started walking closer to the shore.

"Hey Lono, why didn't you show up to the temple that one time?" Bomoh asked.

Lono sighed, "Bomoh, with all due respect, I think we have bigger things to worry about right now." His eyes were fixed on the smaller boat being lowered from the main ship, carrying four or five people.

"Fair enough," Bomoh nodded, understanding the gravity of the situation. They both watched in silence as the boat made its way towards the shore, the people held their breath.

Once the boat was close enough, one of its occupants jumped out to guide it further in. The islanders instinctively made room, forming a large circle around the boat. The elders stepped forward to initiate contact.

"Hello! Can you understand us?" one of the elders called out.

A woman from the boat, dressed in an extravagant gown adorned with sparkling gems and intricate jewelry, stepped forward. She removed her pointed shoes, placing her bare feet in the sand, and approached the elders with a slight bow.

"Yes indeed, I can understand you," she replied with a warm smile.

Lono, eager to hear better, pushed through the crowd to get closer, Bomoh right behind him.

"Do you come in peace?" the elder asked.

"Of course," she chuckled. "You see, we are merely lost."

The woman, perceiving the skepticism etched on the faces of the islanders, decided to address their concerns with a touch of elegance and poise. "I can sense the seeds of doubt planted in your minds, and I must say, your caution is well warranted. However..." she paused gracefully, gesturing towards the vessel she had disembarked from, "Might I direct your attention to my actions, or more precisely, my offerings?"

Her entourage began to carefully unload three containers from the boat, filled with the unknown. The elders shared wary glances, subtly nodding to the island's warriors, prompting them to approach with caution.

Noticing the escalating tension, the woman elegantly raised her arms in a gesture of peace. "Please, hold your advance. I can assure you people, my intentions are devoid of any malice," she proclaimed, her voice resonating with a calm yet commanding presence.

The elders, still guarded but now sensing a genuine sincerity in her words, signaled their warriors to maintain their positions, remaining alert as they awaited the unfolding events.

She approached the container, her gown whispering against the sand as she moved. Kneeling beside it, she lifted the lid with a practiced ease, revealing the treasures inside. The crowd, drawn by the allure of the unknown, craned their necks, standing on tiptoes to get a better view.

"Behold," she said, her voice rich and warm, filling the air as she gestured towards the gems inside. The container was filled with stones that seemed to hold the essence of the stars themselves, patterns swirling across their surfaces in an endless dance. The islanders couldn't help but gasp, their eyes wide with wonder as they took in the sight.

The elders, caught up in the moment, stepped forward, their faces alight with curiosity and admiration. "They're astonishing to look at. So precious," one of them murmured, his eyes not leaving the gems.

"I know." she replied as she turned to the next container, "If you think that over there is impressive, just you wait..."

She lifted the lid, revealing what appeared to be an assortment of colorful, smooth stones. The crowd's reaction was more subdued, their expressions filled with intrigue rather than awe.

"No gasps this time, huh?" she observed, a playful note in her voice as she stood back up. "Boy," she called, pointing to a young child in the crowd, "Come and behold its taste."

The kid's mother, protective instincts kicking in, held him back. "Aw, it's okay. I promise. All the kids back home LOVE to eat these," she reassured, her voice gentle and coaxing.

One of the elders, sensing the mother's apprehension, offered a nod of encouragement. "They clearly come in peace. Why not show them some courtesy?" he suggested, his voice steady and reassuring.

The mother, after a moment's hesitation, released her hold, smiling encouragingly at her son. "Go on," she whispered, her voice filled with a newfound trust.

The kid took cautious steps toward her and the containers. "Come on, it's alright," she said, her voice calm and inviting, a gentle smile playing on her lips.

"What's your name?" she asked, as he finally stood before her.

"Māui," he replied, his voice small yet clear.

"I am Jezebel," she responded, her smile widening just a touch, enough to put Māui at ease.

"And what color might you want?" she inquired.

"Red, I guess..." he muttered.

Reaching into the container, she pulled out a red one and handed it to him. He took it hesitantly, then placed it in his mouth. A hush fell over the crowd as they watched, waiting.

After a few tense seconds, his eyes went wide with delight. He turned to his mother, sharing a look of happiness and relief. "Yummy!" he exclaimed, his voice filled with joy.

A ripple of gentle laughter spread through the islanders, the tension easing. "Can I have some more, please?" he asked, his earlier apprehension replaced with excitement.

"As much as you want," she replied.

"Now! For the last gift of mine!" she announced, her voice carrying across the beach as she relocated over to the last container. But as she prepared to open it, she noticed Māui still standing there, eating happily. "Hey, boy, run along now," she said, tapping his shoulder, guiding him back toward his parents.

With a soft "Hmm..." barely audible, she gathered herself, returning to her previous rhythm. "Behold and come!" she called out, her voice resonant as she gracefully opened the container and reached inside.

When she stood back up, she held a small calf in her arms, its skin shimmering with a golden hue unlike anything the islanders had ever seen. The crowd fell silent, their eyes wide as they took in the sight of the miraculous creature.

With a gentle motion, she placed the golden calf on the ground, watching as it made its way toward one of the elders. He reached down, scooping it up into his arms with a look of admiration on his face.

"What a wonderful looking creature," he commented, bringing the calf closer to his face, examining its golden skin with awe.

"It's an offering from us to you," Jezebel declared, rising to her feet with a grace that didn't go unnoticed.

"I am truly pleased," the elder responded, his voice filled with gratitude. He turned to address the crowd, holding the calf high for all to see. "Will we shut our doors to these lost folks who have shown us nothing but generosity and peace?"

Murmurs of agreement rippled through the crowd, and nods of approval could be seen from the majority of the islanders. Lono, who had been watching the proceedings closely, felt his tension ease, though a hint of hesitation still lingered in his eyes. He glanced over at Bomoh, noting his agreement with the elder's words.

"If I may," Jezebel spoke, her voice steady and composed as it flowed over the crowd, her gaze intently fixed on the three elders. "In a final gesture of my goodwill, we seek only guidance back to our lands. We propose to remain aboard our vessels, sending only a messenger of your choice to communicate between our people and yours. Would this arrangement bring comfort to your people?"

After a brief moment of contemplation, one of the elders stepped forward, his expression thoughtful. "This proposal is agreeable and brings us reassurance," he responded.

Those who had come with Jezebel prepared to return to the main ship, awaiting her signal. She made her way to one of the elders, leaning in to murmur, "Make sure they feast on my gifts. It will mean the world to me."

Before the elder could respond, she turned and walked back toward the boat, her steps measured and her head held high, leaving a lasting impression on the islanders as she departed.

Bomoh turned to Lono with a smile. "Aren't we lucky to not only find more like us but for them to be so kind?" he exclaimed, his voice carrying genuine enthusiasm.

"Yeah..." Lono replied, giving a slight nod. His mind was elsewhere, filled with swirling thoughts.

"I'm going to head back home... I'm sure Laka is worried," he announced, looking away.

"You should bring her one of those rock thingies, or bring her to see that calf," he suggested, excitement evident in his tone.

"Sure...be seeing you later," Lono responded, his voice distant as he began to walk away, preoccupied with his thoughts.

As he ventured back home, Lono couldn't help but replay the events at the shore. Despite the peaceful exchange and the gifts, he was left with lingering doubts and questions. "How come everyone was so fine knowing that we weren't the only ones in the world, as the elders and previous generations stated?" he pondered, slowing his pace as he lost himself in thought.

"And her appearance... the paleness of her skin was odd if she's been at sea, and she was so tall. Definitely going to be a strange story to tell Laka," he mused, chuckling despite his contemplative state.

His journey back was filled with a mixture of awe, skepticism, and a deep sense of wonder about the world beyond his island.

CHAPTER FOUR

TUG OF WAR

Lono pushed open the door to his house, stepping inside. Laka, sensing his arrival, left the back porch and quickly made her way to him, wrapping her arms around him in a warm, comforting hug.

"So everything is okay?" she asked, her voice filled with concern.

"I don't know..." Lono replied, his voice heavy with uncertainty.

"What do you mean you don't know? You made it down there, right?" she pressed.

"Yeah, I made my way to the front and saw everything up close. But even then, something about the whole situation just doesn't sit right with me," he responded, his gaze distant as he settled into the sofa.

She followed, sitting close beside him, her hand finding his in a supportive gesture. "What's wrong, love?" she asked, her voice soft and filled with love.

"They came from the main ship on a smaller boat, bringing containers filled with... 'gifts,' or at least that's what she called them," He began, recounting the events.

"What were the gifts?" She interrupted gently, her curiosity piqued.

"A golden calf, some colorful foods, and some gems," he listed.

"And what did the elders say?" she inquired, eager to understand the whole story. "They told us to show them generosity, since they claimed to be lost or something along those lines," he explained, his skepticism evident in his voice.

"What's your heart telling you?" she asked, looking deep into his eyes, searching for the truth in his emotions.

"Not to trust them at all. Everything about it was odd. The feeling I even got while standing there... was so unknown... as if deep in my soul I had a tug-of-war with her words," he said, meeting her gaze.

"We should tell the elders at once then. Right?" she suggested, a hint of urgency in her voice.

"Honestly, love, I think we should leave this one alone and just do us as we always do," he replied, offering her a reassuring smile.

"Well, you know me. If everything's cool, then we're cool, right?" she chuckled, her mood lightening.

"Now... remember the starving baby? She requires food like now, so sorry, love..." She lunged at him playfully, starting to nibble on him in a playful manner. "You just look so good... yum, yum, yum!" she exclaimed happily.

"Oh, for real???" He opened his mouth wider in mock surprise and began to make munching noises as he nibbled on her neck, joining in the playful banter.

Their laughter filled the room, creating a light-hearted atmosphere. However, she was the first to compose herself, adopting a jokingly serious tone as she said, "We are hungry though."

"Ok, ok," he responded, chuckling as he stood up and made his way to the kitchen to start cooking.

"I cut up everything you needed, I think. Just let me know if I missed anything," she called out, watching as he began to survey the prepped ingredients laid out in the kitchen.

As he turned on the tap to wash his hands, the water flowed out a shocking shade of blood red for a brief moment. "That's new... What the heck..." he muttered aloud, his eyes widening in surprise.

"What now?" she called from the other room, her voice filled with concern.

"The water, just now... It was a hue of red," he explained, still trying to make sense of what he had just seen.

"Let me see," she said, getting up to join him in the kitchen. She reached over, turned off the tap, and then turned it back on again. The water flowed out clear and normal. "Nothing now... Of course," he said, his voice tinged with annoyance.

"Guess I'm just lucky," she remarked, a playful smile on her face.

"Well... whatever. Sorry I made a fuss over nothing," he said, his shoulders slumping slightly as he turned back to the task at hand.

"It's fine, love," she reassured him warmly, dismissing his concerns with a loving tone. Before returning to the sofa, she filled a cup with water.

"Actually, love..." she hesitated as she made her way back into the living room, her nose crinkling in discomfort. "This smells like rotten eggs."

Curious, he walked over to her and took a whiff of the water in her cup. He then relocated to the running tap water and found it had the same foul smell. "That's disgusting," he grimaced.

"Something must have died in the pipes or something, right?" she suggested, trying to make sense of the strange occurrence.

"I don't know," he said, pondering the situation. "We can boil it first and see if that helps."

CHAPTER FIVE

SOMETHING IN THE PIPES

The sun blazed overhead, reaching its zenith and casting a radiant glow over the island. The beach, once thronged with the islanders' curious and cautious bodies, was now sparsely populated. The excitement had dwindled, but its remnants could be seen in the children who were still abuzz with energy from the exotic food they'd sampled.

Among the scattering of people, Bomoh meandered along the shoreline. In his hand, he held one of the mysterious gems, its patterns swirling in a mesmerizing dance. His eyes were locked onto it, his mind seemingly entranced, detached from the world around him.

As he walked, lost in the gem's allure, a child full of life and laughter darted across his path. The unexpected collision sent the child tumbling to the sand.

"Oh, I am sorry, little one..." Bomoh quickly apologized, snapping out of his reverie. He extended a hand to help the child up. "Here."

"Screw you, old man!" the kid retorted with a surprising boldness, brushing off Bomoh's hand as he scrambled to his feet. Without another word, the child dashed off to rejoin his friends, leaving Bomoh standing there with a mixture of surprise and bemusement.

Bomoh was taken aback by the child's brusque remarks. Shaking his head slightly, he turned away from the shore, deciding to head toward the temple. As he walked, a slight headache began to form, a dull pressure at the temples that made him squint against the brightness of the sun.

He cast a glance back at the shore, a sense of unease settling over him for reasons he couldn't quite place. "Perhaps it's just the strain of today's events," he mused internally, attributing his discomfort to the stress and his aging body.

As he continued his walk, the modest but familiar buildings of his small city brought him a comforting familiarity. The temple, a humble structure that stood at the city's heart, was drawing near. It was there that the other shamans were assembling, ready to consult with the elders.

Within the temple, a discussion would soon take place. They would come together to select one among the islanders who would help navigate the visitors back to their own lands.

As Bomoh stepped through the temple door, he immediately noticed the gathered circle already deep in discussion. His arrival broke the flow of their conversation as he made his entrance known.

"Apologies for my tardiness," he announced, moving to find his place among them. "I was sidetracked."

"Oh, that's fine, Brother Bomoh," one of the elders replied with a dismissive wave. "We've already made our choice."

"And who might that be?" Bomoh inquired.

The chief elder spoke up, his voice carrying the weight of authority. "Considering the renown he once held, Lono seemed the obvious choice," he declared, and nods of assent rippled around the room.

Bomoh, taken aback, responded with disbelief, "How so? The man has spent the last year or so cooped up in his house, practically under his wife's skirt." A ripple of laughter followed his remark, affirming the shared sentiment.

In that moment, however, a flicker of self-reflection crossed Bomoh's mind. "Did I really just say that?" The thought surprised him.

"I am sorry, Kane, but is there truly no one else?" Bomoh pressed, addressing the chief elder with a measure of respect in his inquiry.

"It has been decided, Bomoh..." Kane responded with finality. "But come, why don't you sit and partake in some of the delightful treats our guests have brought us?" he suggested, attempting to redirect Bomoh's concern.

Bomoh hesitated, his eyes betraying a hint of reluctance. "If it eases your mind, we've already dispatched the messenger boy to notify Lono. He's likely on his way to the ship as we speak," Kane added with an assuring smile.

"Actually, might I be excused?" Bomoh requested gently, his hand subconsciously drifting to his temple. "This headache seems to be worsening."

"Of course," Kane consented with an understanding nod. "Take care of yourself, be safe out there!" he called out warmly, with the other shamans and elders chiming in with waves and words of parting for Bomoh as he made his exit.

Bomoh stumbled out of the temple, his steps unsteady. Every so often, his balance would falter, sending a spike of concern through his mind. "I definitely need some rest," he murmured to himself.

His own house thankfully close by, offered the promise of rest. This proximity was not a product of his own planning; as he ventured, a smile found him when he thought of his wife. It had been her insistence that they live near the temple, a decision he was profoundly thankful for today more than ever.

Bomoh reached his house. His throat parched, he walked towards the kitchen, seeking the cool relief of water. With a wearied turn of the tap, he awaited the usual rush of liquid, but nothing came. A frown creased his brow as he struck the tap in frustration, yet it remained dry. Bending forward, he peered into the spout for any visible blockage — nothing obstructed the flow.

"That's a..." he began, but his words were abruptly cut short. With a sudden, violent surge, the pipe exploded, spewing forth a torrent of blood. It splashed across his face, blinding him, the shock of it sending him staggering backward. He tumbled to the floor, a sharp pain shooting through his hips and tailbone, his surroundings fading into a murky, bloody haze.

Bomoh tried to regain his bearings, now on all fours, his sight robbed by the viscous blood that clung to his eyes. The pain in his lower body was sharp, too intense to allow him to stand. "Help!" he cried out, his voice echoing off the walls of his own house.

He paused, straining his ears for a response, but there was none — only the sinister sound of the running water continued to invade the silence. With trepidation, he began to crawl, moving cautiously to orient himself. His hand brushed against something unexpectedly wet and slimy, a texture alien to him. Despite his efforts to squint through the blood, visibility remained at naught.

"Please! Can anyone help me?" His voice was tinged with desperation now. The sound of the "water" seemed to amplify.

He halted, sensing a shift in the atmosphere. A giggle, chillingly out of place, sounded in the room, and then the water stopped. "Who's there?" Bomoh demanded, his voice firm despite his helplessness. "Speak at once!" he commanded into the void.

There was no response, no sound to indicate the presence of another. Doubt crept into his mind — was his mind conjuring phantoms now? He had to reach the front door; he had to escape this nightmare. With a mixture of fear and determination, he continued his blind and painful journey across the floor.

As Bomoh's fingertips traced the contours of the wall, his heart pulsed with hope. The door frame's familiar edge brought a surge of relief. His hands scoured the surface frantically for the knob, his movements growing more frenetic with each passing second. The absence of the knob, that crucial point of egress, sparked a fresh wave of panic.

With his heart racing and his mind teetering on the edge of despair, Bomoh found a spark of resolve. It was a spark that flared into determination, an inner strength that he had nurtured through years of spiritual discipline and meditation. Just days ago, he would have turned to his meditation as a reflex, a natural response to any sign of distress. Now, under the shadow of this bizarre and terrifying ordeal, he called upon that practice once more.

Struggling against the throbbing pain in his lower body and the stickiness of blood on his hands and face, Bomoh endeavored to calm his breath. He sought the measured rhythm that had always been the harbinger of tranquility. He pressed his palms together, his fingers pointing upwards in a gesture of seeking balance, and attempted to center his spirit. He sought refuge in his spiritual vision, a realm where the darkness of his physical world could not follow.

The pitch black of his material surroundings gave way to a clarity within the spiritual plane. He could see his own house once again, but his otherworldly sight brought no comfort. Where he expected tranquility, there was turmoil; where he sought solace, there was only despair. His very soul seemed to weep, yearning for nonexistence, a reaction so visceral that his innermost self recoiled in horror.

His thoughts, once a bastion of serenity, were now a maelstrom of fear and self-preservation. In the depths of his being, a primal plea emerged, one that shocked even him. He bargained with the creature that stood in front of him. "TAKE ANYTHING. PLEASE, TAKE MY WIFE AND KIDS! TAKE IT ALL, but spare me!" The very essence of who he was seemed to fracture under the weight of this terror, as he sought to trade all he had ever loved for a break from this inexplicable horror.

CHAPTER SIX

THE OFFERING

A knock sounded at the door. Lono and Laka were seated at their table, immersed in their meal, when Laka shook her head, silently suggesting they ignore the interruption. Another knock came, harder this time.

"Folks really can't eat in peace today, huh?" Lono said, his voice tinged with irritation.

"Want me to get it?" Laka offered, ready to stand.

"Nah... I got it," Lono replied, taking another bite of his food before reluctantly getting up. The knocking persisted, each thud louder and more demanding. "Hey man! I'm coming!" Lono raised his voice in response, his annoyance clear.

Laka turned her attention to the front door, muttering under her breath about the persistence of their visitor. "They're trying to break the dang thing down."

"Right!?" Lono agreed, his affirmation echoed by the creak of the door hinges as it swung open, revealing Bomoh standing on the other side.

"Bomoh?" Laka said, her tone a mix of disbelief and concern.

"Hello, Laka. Been quite..." Bomoh began, but before he could finish, Lono had stepped outside, closing the door behind him, shielding Laka from Bomoh's view. Bomoh looked up at Lono, his expression blank, devoid of the emotions one would expect in such a reunion.

Lono's gaze was unwavering, his stance firm as he addressed Bomoh. "I know you're a man of stature and all, but my patience is wearing thin," Lono said, his irritation evident. "My apologies, I never meant to..." Bomoh started, but Lono cut him off. "What is it now?" Lono demanded.

"You've been chosen to be the bridge between us and the outsiders," Bomoh revealed, a small smile flickering across his face, perhaps in an attempt to ease the tension.

"Under whose authority?" Lono questioned.

"The decision was unanimous. Even Kane agreed," Bomoh responded, hoping to convey the gravity of the elders' consensus.

Lono weighed Bomoh's words. He knew this was not a request to be taken lightly.

Lono exhaled deeply, the weight of the unexpected duty settling on his shoulders. "How soon?" he inquired.

"Today... right now would be preferable," Bomoh replied, his smile gentle.

Lono shook his head, a mix of disbelief and resignation in his eyes. "Let me finish my meal, at least," he said, his tone a blend of irritation and acquiescence.

Bomoh nodded, understanding. "You'll do great, Lono," he encouraged.

"A washed-up fisherman? Who am I to guide anyone?" Lono replied, half in jest, half in earnest.

"No, Lono. You've been a beacon to this land, and you will be so again," Bomoh reassured him, bowing slightly to signal his departure. "Have a good day," he finished, leaving Lono to his thoughts and his unfinished meal.

Lono re-entered the house, the door closing softly behind him. Laka was right where he left her, her expression a mix of concern and curiosity. "Did I just hear him say you're the one they're sending to talk to those strangers?" she asked.

"Yep..." Lono replied, sinking back into his chair. He picked up his spoon, pausing as he looked at her. "Should I even go through with this?" he questioned.

"You know I'm not about you jumping into anything wild... and this is about as wild as it gets," Laka responded.

"Today's been a series of crazy, that's for sure," he agreed, finally taking another bite.

"What if you just... lie to them?" she suggested quietly.

"What?" Lono looked up, surprised.

"Think about it. You could point them in a direction, say that's where you saw land once," she proposed.

Lono chewed thoughtfully for a moment. "I don't know. What if that just makes them angry? What if they decide to retaliate?" he pondered aloud.

"Good point. And we might be sending good people to their doom if they're actually lost," Laka added, a tinge of sadness in her voice.

"Yeah..." Lono sighed, setting down his fork. "The idea did cross my mind, but maybe that's just us wanting to stay out of it, to be together." He offered her a wry smile.

She returned the smile, albeit faintly. "Yeah, I know."

They both resumed eating, the silence comfortable between them. "How long do you think it'll take?" she finally broke the quiet.

"Not sure. Hopefully, I'll be back before sunset if I leave soon. Depends on what the elders want from their messenger boy," he said with a chuckle.

Laka shook her head in silent agreement to the absurdity of the situation. They lingered over their meal, savoring the flavors and the fleeting moments of normalcy.

With the meal concluded and their conversation ebbing to a natural pause, Lono glanced out the window, noting the position of the sun. It was descending, but still generous with its light, offering him a few more hours of day to navigate the unknown task ahead.

He stood, collecting the dishes, his movements slow, almost reluctant. She watched him, her eyes tracing the familiar lines of his face, etching this ordinary moment into memory. They shared glances, an unspoken acknowledgment of the challenges that lay later that day.

With the last of the plates gathered, he moved towards the door. She followed, their steps in quiet tandem.

Standing by the open door, the boundary between the warmth of their home and the world outside felt stark. He turned to her. "Time to go," he finally said, his voice steady but soft. She nodded, her smile a mixture of pride and concern.

"Bye love," he said, planting a kiss on her lips, then bending to press another against the swell of her belly. "Just you wait until you're out here," he teased, speaking to the baby.

"Hey! What do you mean by that? She's good out here in these streets," Laka retorted playfully, her maternal instinct wrapped in humor.

Lono raised his hands in mock surrender. "I see how it is. But she's still gonna owe me for all the food she's been taking from me," he laughed.

"You're gonna get beat up," Laka warned, her jesting tone belying the depth of her affection.

His laughter faded as his expression sobered, the weight of the impending task casting a shadow over his features. "Be seeing you soon," he said, a promise and a hope as he stepped out into the uncertainty that awaited him.

Chapter Seven

THE BEACON

As Lono descended the hill towards the temple, glimpses of the ships peeked through the gaps between the houses, stark reminders of the task at hand. With each step, his mind raced, strategizing responses for potential turmoil. Silently, he sent prayers to the land, seeking protection for his wife and a rekindling of the courage that had once been second nature to him. His heart, once a drumbeat to the rhythm of the waves, had grown quiet in the stillness of domestic life; a stillness that, in these pressing times, felt like a dormant strength he now longed to awaken.

As Lono approached the temple's entrance, he paused, drawing in a deep breath. Pushing the door open, he was met with an unexpected sight: elders and shamans moving in unfamiliar, almost erratic dances around a golden calf that seemed unnaturally enlarged since he last saw it.

"Hello?" His voice echoed slightly, uncertainty lacing the word. The dancing ceased abruptly, all eyes turning to him. An uncomfortable silence hung in the air until Lono, unable to stand the quiet, spoke again. "Y'all good?"

"Of course!" The response came from Kane, who emerged from the group and approached Lono with a welcoming smile. "Glad you made it here so fast."

"Yeah..." Lono replied, his gaze drifting past Kane to the others, who were frozen in strange postures. Kane, noticing Lono's distracted squint, subtly shifted to block the view and placed a hand on Lono's shoulder, steering him back towards the door.

"Look, Lono. We want you to take this scroll up to them..." Kane began, guiding Lono outside. As the doors swung shut behind them, Lono caught a final glimpse of the motionless figures inside, their stares unnervingly fixed on him, so still they seemed frozen in time.

"Alright. So, after this, I'm good, right? No more running up and down?" Lono asked, looking for confirmation that this task would be the last.

"These scrolls are everything they need to know; it should be the only trip," Kane replied, giving Lono a reassuring nod. "Feeling anxious?" he inquired, noticing the slight edge in Lono's voice.

"Nah," Lono said, extending his hand to receive the scrolls. Kane handed them over, their age evident in the delicate parchment and the gleam of the golden seal. "Thank you once more, Lono," Kane said, his smile conveying gratitude.

Lono nodded, clutching the scrolls, and turned to walk towards the shore. Glancing upwards, he noted the rapid descent of the sun. "Yep... Today sucks," he mused silently.

"Hey, Lono, before I forget!" Kane called out, his pace quickening as he approached Lono. "Once you're at the shore, you must light the standing torch we've set up for you," he said, slightly winded.

"Why?" Lono inquired, a crease forming between his brows.

"You won't be using your boat; they will come for you," Kane explained, catching his breath.

"Thanks," Lono responded with a nod, though his frustration was barely veiled.

"Anything else I should know?" he asked, his tone edged with a hint of impatience.

"No, that's everything, "Kane assured him before turning to make his way back to the temple.

Arriving at the shore, Lono was struck by the eerie stillness that hung over the area. It was a striking difference to the usual vibrancy of celebration that the day typically held. Memories of past festivities flickered in his mind—the roaring fires, the feasts, and the laughter he shared with his wife on these sands.

He cast his gaze out to sea, where the silhouettes of the ships loomed in the distance. As he watched, a smaller boat began to make its way toward the shore, drawn to the beacon of the lit torch where Lono stood, a solitary figure against the vastness of the ocean.

The boat's outline cut through the twilight as the sun dipped below the horizon, surrendering the sky to the encroaching night. Clouds amassed overhead, heavy with the promise of a storm, the air thick with its impending arrival. Lono squinted, trying to discern the figure rowing the boat. It was one of the same individuals who had earlier handled the containers, their attire ragged in incongruity to the woman's neat appearance.

For the first time, Lono realized he hadn't seen their faces; they rowed with heads bowed, as if in deference or shame. A chill of unease crept up his spine, his instincts flaring to life with every stroke that brought the boat closer. Memories of the day's oddities flashed through his mind—warnings he had dismissed or overlooked, as though he had been compelled to ignore them.

Then, abruptly, a sharp pain lanced through his head, so intense it brought him to his knees. He clutched at his skull, the scrolls slipping from his grasp to the sand below, as he grunted in anguish.

He pressed his fingers to his temples, trying to ease the hammering pain as his heart raced, pumping adrenaline through his veins. The thud in his head was matched only by the steady, advancing steps of the stranger walking from the shore. Step by step, heartbeat by heartbeat, they were in tandem—a stark, rhythmic reminder of the urgency of the moment. The last step came just as another pulse echoed in his skull, the figure now standing beside him.

In the span of a halted heartbeat, Lono's world slowed to an imperceptible crawl. He felt each grain of sand as they shifted beneath his fingers, a dance of minute tremors that whispered of a deeper turmoil.

The cries of the sand grew louder in his ears, a cacophony of tiny voices that swelled to fill the space of his paused reality. It was then, with the clarity of a serene yet piercing note in the silence, that Lono understood—it was not merely the sand that called out but all around, the soil and stone of his home an ethereal chorus of the land itself in anguish.

Time, which had hung suspended now ticked forward, resuming its steady march. The grip of the headache that had commandeered his senses began to wane, the oppressive weight lifting, allowing the sharpness of reality to seep back in. His focus sharpened, and his eyes, now clearing, caught sight of a hand that reached for the scrolls. It was a canvas of scars and burns, its story one not of valor, but of survival through torment. Marks that could be mistaken for battle scars were in truth the cruel imprints of captivity and punishment.

Lono's reflexes snapped, his hand shooting out to seize the scroll before the stranger could. His action sent the other's hand recoiling in a startled arc. Rising with the parchment clutched tightly, Lono locked gazes with the figure before him.

In that gaze, Lono found a tapestry of fear and deformity—a face marred not by nature but by cruel intent, lips forcibly silenced by rough, threaded stitches. He dropped to his knees. His eyes, wide with a silent plea, implored Lono for the scrolls.

With a gentle touch, Lono whispered, "I am sorry, but I can't," his voice as firm as it was soft. The stranger felt a sense of ease when Lono touched him and for the first time he closed his eyes without the fear of retaliation.

In that fleeting connection, histories interwove; the stranger's origins, once shrouded in obscurity, now lay bare. He was home. Yet, with this revelation, Lono's heart only harbored a growing fury.

Lono eased his grasp on the stranger's hand and turned his attention to the scroll. With a careful flick of his wrist, he unfurled the parchment, and his eyes scanned the contents. There, listed in a meticulous script, were names familiar to him—names of those who called his city home. Understanding dawned, and without a second thought, he ripped the scroll in two, letting the pieces flutter down to the sand. As the fragments settled, the wind seemed to carry away the weight of those inked words.

Meanwhile, the stranger, still silent, seized handfuls of sand, his tears a mingling of joy and sorrow. He was home, yet the specter of retribution loomed large. As joy for his return battled the dread of punishment, the scales tipped — for now, home was winning. His two companions abandoned the boat and raced to his side.

Lono turned; his gaze fixed on the distant ships. His stride was purposeful, unswayed by doubt or fear. In his heart, a mantra pulsed with every step—'Keep your family safe.' This wasn't just a thought; it was a pledge, a father's oath that coursed through him, as inevitable as the tide.

Lono, with determined strides, embarked upon the small vessel that would carry him across the waters to the looming silhouette of the main ship. As the shoreline receded with each pull of the oars, he cast a lingering glance over his shoulder, beholding the familiar expanse of his homeland. The view was one ingrained in his memory from countless days spent casting nets into the generous sea.

Beyond the immediate reach of sight, where the land cradled his dwelling, an image of his wife surfaced in his mind's eye, vivid and endearing. He saw her as she was on their wedding day, radiant and with child, her promise of "Forever and Always" echoing through time to caress his spirit. It had been a day of unbridled joy, the memory of which now formed a stark contrast against the backdrop of his current quest.

With the past cradling his resolve, Lono faced forward once more, the dark mass of the ship casting a long shadow upon the water, enveloping him. He was now under its great bulk, a lone figure standing on the brink of the unknown, the silent whispers of his heart's vows propelling him onward.

CHAPTER EIGHT

FOREVER & ALWAYS

Lono's hands gripped the rope, coarse and familiar against his calloused skin. With each pull, his muscles, honed from years of casting nets and battling the capricious ocean, remembered their old strength. He ascended swiftly, more swiftly than he'd anticipated, the urgency of his task lending him vigor he figured.

Reaching the top, his eyes scanned his new surroundings, falling on a sight that was both unexpected and unsettling. There, seated atop a barrel as though she had anticipated his arrival, was the tall woman.

Jezebel's appearance had transformed since Lono's last encounter with her. Gone was the opulent gown that spoke of her authority and wealth. In its place, she donned a robe, the fabric of which was deceptively modest in volume yet daring in its disclosure, threatening to reveal the secrets it lazily guarded with every subtle shift of her body.

Her legs were encased in a mesh of intricate weave, akin to the nets Lono had used to harvest the bounty of the sea, yet these were not meant for fishing. The material clung to her skin, each strand a delicate contour mapping her form in a way that was almost hypnotic. It was an attire that seemed to mock the utility of the very nets that sustained Lono and his people, repurposed into a symbol of perversion.

Jezebel rose from her reclined position, a smirk playing on her lips. "Finally," she murmured, her voice a blend of satisfaction and anticipation.

"Finally what!" Lono's voice thundered across the deck, his anger raw and demanding. "What have you done?" He demanded.

In response, Jezebel offered only a silent appraisal. Her gaze traveled the length of Lono's form, an unspoken challenge, measuring his resolve. Then, with a slow, deliberate motion, she drew her tongue over her bright red lips, a bold, unnerving gesture that disregarded his anger, as if savoring the anticipation of an unspoken game only she understood.

"Ah, the visage I so fondly recall," She said, her fingers delicately tracing the edge of her white robe. With a calculated grace, she let the garment slide away.

His anger surged at the sight before him, his jaw tightening. "Come and behold," she beckoned with an outstretched hand, a twisted invitation hanging in the tense air between them.

She began to speak again, "It's our—"

"NO!" His voice erupted in a defiant roar, a force unbeknownst even to himself. In an instant, silence; the next, a concussive blast reverberated through the ship, propelling her back with a violent gust, her back slamming against the ship's wall. The sheer power of his cry rippled through the air, the shockwave reaching the distant shorelines and sending the waters into a tempestuous dance.

His stance remained unshaken, his posture a testament to the confusion that furrowed his brow. He glanced at his own hand, expecting some arcane transformation or the shimmer of a spiritual veil—but there was none. His hand was firm and real.

As he took a moment of introspection, the woman recomposed herself with unsettling ease. Muscles extended in a lithe stretch, fingers and neck popping in a symphony of readiness. "So this is your curse," she declared audibly to Lono, a sly grin forming on her lips. "Let me show you my blessings," she announced before launching into motion—a blur to Lono's unaccustomed eyes. The force of her punch buried itself in his midsection, robbing him of both breath and balance. But before he could succumb to the blow's full momentum, her right hand ensnared his hair, yanking him from the flight path. Then, with a swift and cruel grace, her left hand came down, slapping him viciously to the ground. The speed and precision of her attack left no room for him to grasp the reality of his new adversary's capabilities.

His head struck the wooden deck, a sickening echo of impact mingling with the brief bounce of skull on hard timber. As he fought through the haze of pain, an instinctive urge to unleash another scream rose within him. But in the fragile moment his mouth gaped open, darkness smothered his senses—a third, thunderous blow from the woman's hand landed, driving his head into the wood and leaving a splintered dent as testament to the force. Her voice, cold and mocking, cut through the thud of the assault.

"Hush, boy," she chuckled.

Lono, drifting in and out of consciousness, was defenseless as the woman began to pry at his clothing with a disturbing grin carving her features. In the midst of his dazed state, he felt the intrusion and summoned the dregs of his strength to resist. As his mind clawed back to awareness, he managed to land a knee firmly against her head, sending her staggering back, a momentary reprieve from her advance.

Pushing her off, he gasped for air, his chest heaving as reality fully set in. She looked down at him, her expression twisting into a malevolent sneer. "Why must you make this so hard?" she said, with venomous annoyance.

Drawing in a deep, grounding breath, his chest swelled with a fury that transcended the physical plane. With a primal scream, he released a concussive blast so potent it tore through the very heart of the ship. The wooden planks splintered and burst asunder, creating a gaping maw in the vessel's side. The woman, caught in the raw force of his outcry, was hurled like a ragdoll across the expanse of dark water, her form a fleeting shadow against the moonlit sky until she crashed onto the beach shore, a considerable distance away, where the sand and the night bore silent witness to her unceremonious descent.

He collapsed, the strain of his newfound power coursing through his veins like poison. His knees hit the deck hard, and he clutched at his throat, the taste of iron flooding his mouth as blood mingled with spit. His breaths were ragged, the effort of unleashing such force leaving him teetering on the brink of collapse.

Forcing himself to look beyond the pain, his eyes slowly adjusted to the ship's carnage. As the minutes ticked by, he gathered his strength and pushed to his feet. The sight that met him cut deeper than any physical wound.

The ship's hold was exposed by a vast rupture from Lono's shout. Men, women, and children, their skin marked by the suns of many lands, were shackled to crude bunks. They were packed in layers, a grotesque parody of a barracks, bound not only by iron but by the thick air of despair. His heart thundered, not with the power that had just surged through him, but with a surge of purpose. He knew he couldn't let this stand. Not now, not ever. She had to die for sure.

CHAPTER NINE

EMPTY PROMISES

Racing back to shore, Lono saw the three strangers from earlier, now perched on the sand, their expressions a mix of shock and disbelief as they beheld their battered master clawing at the earth, smeared with blood and grit.

Wading through the cold embrace of the water, Lono made his way to land with determined steps. Lifting his gaze, he saw a growing crowd drawn by the clamor of his explosive shout. Their lanterns flickered like fireflies, casting a warm glow over the beach and highlighting the collective curiosity on their faces.

"One last time, woman. What is it you want?" Lono's voice boomed across the shore, ensuring every gathered soul could bear witness to this confrontation.

She ceased her laborious crawling, resigning to lie on her back as the life ebbed from her body. An attempt to laugh turned into a fit of coughing, spattering blood upon the sand. Her eyes, growing dim, locked with Lono's, standing over her.

"Love...ly wife..." she gasped, the words barely a whisper, as a final, unsettling smile curled the edges of her lips. In her passing, an eerie silence descended, a stark contrast to the tumultuous scream that had just shattered the night.

The throng near the shore seemed disoriented, many clutching their heads as if emerging from a deep fog, their consciousness clawing back to clarity. Lono turned away from the haunting scene, the woman's final smile etched in his memory, her last words echoing in his skull. With a sense of urgency propelling him, he began to run toward his home. Each stride was laden with a desperate need to ensure the safety of his family, to return to them, to protect them from whatever malevolence had just been laid to rest on the beach.

His hand pressed against the door, easing it open with a restraint born of caution. The darkness within seemed to swallow even the ambient sounds of the night, leaving only the thumping of his own pulse in his ears as a companion.

Then, a sound cut through the silence, the unmistakable clatter of hooves—rapid and rhythmic, emanating from the direction of his room. His earlier caution cast aside by the urgency clawing at his chest, he moved swiftly to his room. His hand reached for the door, and with a swift push, he prepared himself for the sight that awaited.

The room lay in dim moonlight, the open shutters allowing a gentle breeze to stir the still air. His eyes quickly adjusted, focusing on the figure in the bed. His wife was there, her body shivering, contorted by the grip of a silent nightmare. Her face, even in distress, a reminder of all the tranquil nights they'd shared, now twisted in fear. His heart tightened, and he approached the bed, reaching out with tenderness, he whispered for her.

Her eyes fluttered open, a mix of confusion and lingering fear clouding their usual warmth. "Lono?" she murmured, her voice hoarse, as if she'd been calling out in her sleep.

"It's me love." He said softly, brushing a strand of hair from her damp forehead. "You okay?"

"You okay?" he asked.

"I think so..." She replied, her voice tinged with uncertainty.

"I'm sorry, love," She said, her arms encircling him in a hug.

"No, I am the one who's sorry..." His voice broke as he spoke. "I left you alone..." Tears began to stream down his face.

"Please..." He choked out, but she cut him off.

"It's okay, love," she soothed, drawing back slightly to cup his face gently in her hands. "We'll be fine. We always find a way, right?" She smiled.

His burdened gaze softened, his head leaning into the solace of her touch, the night's harrowing events momentarily eased.

"We need to go," He said, urgency sharpening his voice.

"Where to?" Laka inquired, her confusion apparent in the dim moonlight filtering through the open window.

"Back to shore and then the temple," he replied. The weight of the night's events pressed upon his words, lending them gravity.

Laka's gaze lingered on his face, seeking understanding. "There's a lot that happened today, especially tonight. I am not going anywhere without you now," he continued, a firm resolve underlying his tone.

She offered him a tender, reassuring smile, her hand finding his in the darkness. "Hey. I might be lost, but I'll always follow you, love," she said.

As she tried to move out of the bed she noticed that the bed was wet and after a second later she felt much lighter. "Baby!" She said in a panic. "Lights please!" Lono rushed to grab one of the lanterns that were hanging in the living room wall. Once lit he rushed his way back to the room illuminating it.

As the lantern's glow filled the space, Lono's eyes were drawn not to his wife, but to the upper corner of the window where a sinister presence loomed. It was a bizarre figure at the window. It had the curved horns of a goat, spiraling into the air with an eerie elegance. Its face was disturbingly bovine, like that of a calf, yet there was a twisted, sentient expression that seemed far too knowing, too cunning for a mere animal.

Blood-red eyes, unsettlingly human in their shape and intelligence, fixated on Laka with an intensity that felt almost invasive. As Lono's gaze intercepted the creature's, a silent exchange passed between them, a moment of recognition that sent a jolt of alarm through him. With a swift, almost bashful movement, the creature withdrew, disappearing from view as if it were reluctant to end the perverse peeping but knew it had been seen.

The terror that gripped him rooted him to the spot. The intense, blood-red gaze of the creature lingered in his mind, a visceral reminder of a menace he had felt in less tangible ways before. But never had it been so close, so personal, and so alarmingly focused on what he held most dear.

His wife's cries became distant as if he were underwater, her panic muffled as his hearing faded into nothingness.

Chapter Ten

A NEW HORIZON

The sun had journeyed across the sky countless times since the night that reshaped their lives, but for Lono and Laka, the shadows of that evening stretched far longer than the passage of days. Lono, once celebrated for his bountiful catches and deft hand with the net, now held a different kind of esteem in the eyes of his community. He had become their liberator, the man who had torn through darkness and despair to restore their freedom. Yet this newfound reverence did nothing to ease the sorrow that had nested in his and Laka's hearts.

Everywhere they went, the looks they received were tinged with a complexity of emotions: gratitude, awe, and a somber recognition of the cost at which their freedom had come. It wasn't triumph that was mirrored in the gazes of their people, but a weighted acknowledgment of the deep loss and the haunting memories that clung to their saviors.

Lono and Laka moved among their people like specters of their former selves, their vibrant spirits dimmed. Their ordeal had not ended with the breaking of chains or the defeat of a menacing foe. It lingered in every silent meal, in every whispered conversation, and in the empty spaces of their home—a home that once rang with the promise of a growing family, now quieted by a profound absence.

They were learning to navigate this new reality, where their roles as heroes felt hollow against the backdrop of their personal anguish.

The betrayal of the elders left a scar that would mark the soul of the community for generations to come. They had been respected, looked upon as guardians of tradition and wisdom, but their heinous acts had revealed a darkness that was now impossible to ignore. The gravity of their deceit weighed heavily on the people and the collective grief and rage found expression in a grim verdict: death for those who had sold their brethren into bondage.

As for Bomoh, there was no trace. The absence of their baby, too, was a wound that refused to heal, an open question that hung in the air like a curse. The lack of any sign, any clue, any droplet of blood to suggest a violent end, only deepened the torment. It was as if the earth itself had swallowed any evidence of their child's fate, leaving Lono and Laka to grapple with an agony devoid of closure.

Today was different, yet hauntingly familiar. He had been harboring an idea, a silent whisper in the back of his mind since that harrowing night. The sea called to him with a siren's allure, tempting him with the thought of chasing the horizon where the strange woman's lands might lie. Could their baby be there?

His gaze was fixed outside the back window, observing his wife as she sat on the porch, her eyes reflecting the boundless ocean before her. Memories cascaded through his mind—vivid flashes of happier times, the weight of a good catch in his nets, the warmth of shared laughter, the softness of her touch. Each recollection was a pulse of aching for what they had lost, for the simplicity and bliss that now seemed worlds away.

A solitary tear traced his weathered cheek, dissolving into the salt on his lips. The story of Lono, the great fisherman, the reluctant hero, ended not with triumph, but with the quiet, briny taste of regret.

About the author

CRISTIAN CARRINGTON

I'm Cristian Carrington, host of The Talking Hour Podcast and a writer with a passion for crafting engaging narratives. With each word I write, I strive to evoke emotions that resonate and offer new perspectives.

This book, while a work of fiction, carries a dedication that is deeply real and personal—it is dedicated to my wife. Her support and belief in my work illuminate my path as a writer. It is with gratitude and love that I share this story with you.

Dive into the second of a captivating five-part short story series! While the grand fantasy novel awaits its unveiling, these tales offer a glimpse into its world. Not direct continuations, but its myths and legends.

Thank you for joining me on this adventure. I hope as you turn each page, you are drawn ever deeper into the worlds I have loved creating.

Also by

The Dance Under The Moonlight

In a mystical, frozen realm, the tribe led by the extraordinary Idun thrived in harmony with nature. Born amidst mysterious omens, Idun's unparalleled abilities transformed her from a defiant young huntress to the tribe's visionary leader. But when she discovers an enigmatic trail leading to an unknown place, it sets off a chain of events that culminate in a heart-wrenching sacrifice as she confronts a formidable foe to protect her people. Dive into this captivating tale of bravery, mystery, and the indomitable spirit of a leader whose legend transcends time. A must-read short tale waiting to be unraveled.

Dive into the first of a captivating five-part short story series! While the grand fantasy novel awaits its unveiling, these tales offer a glimpse into its world. Not direct continuations, but its myths and legends.